Their

a Tales of Moonspell novel

Jessica Coulter Smith

Other Books by Jessica Coulter Smith

Whispering Lake

Magnolia Magick

Eternally Mine

Yuletide Spirit

Night's Embrace

Luna Werewolves series

Vicus Luna (Book 1)

Books in the Ashton Grove Series

Moonlight Protector (Book 1)

Moonlight Hero (Book 2)

Moonlight Guardian (Book 3)

Moonlight Champion (Book 4)

Moonlight Savior (Book 5)

Vaaden Captives

Sorcha

Enid

Susan

Vaaden Warriors

Rheul

Randar

Thale

Short Stories

For Now and Always

Creole Nights

Love at First Bite

Chapter One

Sin stared at the three sticks on her bathroom counter in disbelief. If they were to be believed, she didn't have the flu, she had a baby, or she would in about eight months. And since her sex life had been rather lacking in the last six months, she knew exactly who to blame for her predicament -- Oran and Night Blaylock. Not that a ménage was a normal thing for her, but she was willing to try anything once. And boy had it been worth it -- well, until now. If her parents could see her now, that is if they hadn't kicked her out when she was eighteen, she imagined they'd say "Sincerity Parker, what have you done now?" or something to that effect.

She still remembered her night with the Blaylock brothers like it was yesterday, had relived it in her mind a thousand times.

* * *

Night's mouth seared hers, claiming her, leaving her weak in the knees. Oran, pressed against her back, nuzzled her neck and nipped gently at her shoulder. She placed shaky hands on Night's broad chest, feeling the steady thump of his heart, the crisp hair tickling her palms.

Oran's arm wrapped around her waist and pulled her back against his hard cock. Her pussy was so wet she was dripping; she wanted them more than she'd ever wanted anyone before. Night's erection pulsed against her belly and she reached down to take him in hand.

Both brothers were large, but then she hadn't expected anything less of men who were well over six feet and broad as a barn. Her hand could barely wrap all the way around his cock and just the thought of that long, thick hardness made her want to beg to be taken. She felt Oran rub against her back and she moaned.

"Have I told you how sexy this is?" Oran asked, caressing the cherry blossom tree tattoo that took up her entire back. He trailed kisses down her spine and softly bit her ass.

She gasped and looked over her shoulder.

"Turn her around, Night."

Before she had time to grasp what was happening, she'd been turned and Oran had pulled her legs over his shoulders and buried his face in her pussy. Night braced her upper body as his brother licked, sucked, and teased her to climax, not once but twice. His tongue had thrust inside of her before lapping at her clit, making her skin hum and her body feel hot, so very hot. His tongue had flicked over her clit before thrusting inside of her, over and over again. She'd thought she couldn't take any more when the first orgasm hit her and almost immediately it rolled into a second one.

Still in a fog from coming so hard, all she could do was cling to Night when he lifted her in his arms and carried her to the bed. They'd opted for a motel near the bar where she worked, none of them certain they could make it any further without tearing each other's clothes off. They'd barely cleared the door before both men had stripped and began undressing Sin.

"Have you ever had two men at once?" Night asked.

She shook her head.

"Has anyone ever fucked your ass before?" Oran asked, looking hopeful.

"No," she said softly.

"Pity," he murmured. "I don't think I can be gentle tonight. But maybe next time we can try that."

Next time? Her heart pounded. She hadn't expected anything more than a one-night stand. Did they think this was the start of something more? Could she handle it if it was? She wasn't sure that's what she wanted now, even with the gorgeous men taking her to dizzying heights. Sin didn't trust easily. A one-night stand was one thing, seeing each other on a regular basis was something different.

Oran stretched out beside her, fondling her breasts and leaning down to take her nipple in his mouth. While he distracted her, Night knelt between her legs, his cock brushing against her pussy. She knew he had to feel how wet she was, how ready, and wondered why he hadn't taken her already. She didn't think she could withstand any teasing, not when she wanted him so badly. If they wanted to go a second round, they could take things slowly then, but right now she needed them fast and hard. She wasn't quite sure how it was going to work with both of them loving her. She just knew she wanted them both.

"Night, please," she begged. "I need you."

She buried her hands in Oran's hair and held him to her breast, arching against him, wanting more of his sweet torture. As Night eased his cock inside of her, she gasped in both pleasure and pain. She'd never been with anyone so well-endowed before and he was stretching her to the max, but it felt oh so good. When he was buried inside of her, she wrapped her legs around his waist, tilting her hips to take him in further.

Night groaned and began thrusting with long, deep strokes. As he fucked her good and hard, Oran kissed her, his tongue tangling with hers, stealing her breath from her lungs. His deep kisses drugged her, left her reeling. His hands plucked at her nipples, increasing her pleasure as Night fucked her. Oran moved to take her nipples in his mouth again, teasing first one and then the other. She felt herself climbing higher and higher. She didn't think she could take much more pleasure, but he proved her wrong. As he kissed her, nibbling at her lips and thrusting his tongue deep, his fingers stroked her clit. It was too much and yet not enough. She felt so hot and so tight, every nerve in her body screaming for release, and then it happened, she bowed off the bed, coming harder than she ever had before. She'd swear she saw stars as she came back down from her high.

"God, I need you, baby," Oran groaned. "I want to be in that sweet pussy, but I don't know that I can wait."

She reached for him, stroking his cock. "Then come up here and let me taste you."

Without needing to be told twice, he knelt by her face and fed her his cock. Her lips stretched wide to accommodate him. The musky scent of him and salty taste had her moaning in pleasure. She sucked hard as he fucked her mouth. With both men pounding into her, she felt herself spiraling out of control, and then she felt it happening again, that loss of control and she knew she was close. When she let go, she nearly blacked out from the intensity of her orgasm. Night roared his pleasure as he entered her one last time and a moment later Oran came in her mouth, his seed bathing her throat as she swallowed every drop.

"Fuck!" Night ran his hands through his hair as he pulled out. "I didn't use a condom."

Her eyes widened. She knew they'd been frantic to be together, but still. She'd thought surely he would remember something like that. "How could you forget something that important?"

"Don't worry, we're both clean," he assured her.

"So am I."

"Please tell me you're on the pill."

She glanced between him and Oran then back again. It wasn't her fertile time so it was doubtful that she'd end up pregnant. And while he was just as much responsible for birth control as she was, she wasn't about to tell him she wasn't on the pill.

"Don't worry. It's fine," she told him.

He nodded. "It isn't that I'm holding you responsible for what happened, I just don't think any of us needs an unplanned pregnancy right now."

Oran retrieved a warm, wet washcloth from the bathroom and cleaned her. She blushed at the

11

intimacy, ridiculous after what they'd just shared. Now came the awkward part. The "thank you for the lovely fuck but I have to go" part, unless of course they wanted more. She was almost relieved when Night started pulling on his clothes and she did the same. Not that another round wouldn't have been enjoyable, but Night's outburst had killed the mood and she wasn't sure she wanted to stick around.

"Well, it's been interesting, guys, but I need to get home." She cleared her throat and paused at the door. "Guess I'll see you around."

Without waiting for a response, she slipped out the door and hurried down the street to the bar. There was always someone there willing to give her a ride home. It was stupid of her not to have a car in a small town that didn't have public transportation, but she really couldn't afford one.

Glancing over her shoulder one last time, making sure they weren't following her, she stepped inside the bar and immediately became lost in the crowd. There was just one thing on her mind. Where had their tattoos come from? She knew the marks on their upper arms hadn't been there when they'd first

12

stripped. They'd appeared at some time during their... what? She couldn't call it making love. Fucking? Seemed crude, but that's pretty much what it was.

Something niggled at the back of her mind, something her friend Griff had once said about werewolves and tattoos, but she couldn't quite grasp it. She let go of the memory with a shrug. It wasn't important.

* * *

"Damn it! What the hell am I supposed to do now?" she wondered.

With a sigh, she debated on whether or not she should try to reach the guys and tell them. She'd hardly seen them since their one night together. They'd been in a few times the week following, had even tried to talk to her a time or two. They insisted it was important, but had been scarce ever since. She wasn't sure if they'd just tired of the bar scene, tired of her, or had gotten busy with life. They hadn't exactly showered her with their attention and affection after their one night together. After two failed attempts at conversations, they'd pretty much left her alone. But honestly, she hadn't known what to say to them. She wasn't used to men coming back for seconds, having never been in a relationship before. Whatever the reason for their absence, she had no way of contacting them unless someone at the bar knew them better than she did. Well, that wasn't entirely true. She could always ask their alpha.

Starting the shower, she stripped out of her pajamas and stepped under the warm spray. She scrubbed her hair and body and then stood under the water, letting it relax her muscles and wash away the morning's stress. She didn't know much about being pregnant, but she did know that stress wasn't good for the baby. She didn't know how she would afford it, but she definitely needed to make an appointment to see a doctor.

It wasn't until the water turned cold that she got out. Dressing in low-rise jeans and a cropped tank top, she put on a little make-up, slipped on her shoes, and headed out the door. It was morning for her, but it was late afternoon for everyone else and the bar was about to open. If she didn't start walking now, she'd be late for work.

As she walked down the broken sidewalk, she took a good look at her neighborhood. Trash littered the street, graffiti decorated every building, sagging fences surrounded dilapidated houses, and thugs hung out on corners. Moonspell was a nice town, but even nice towns had a bad element, and she lived right in the middle of it. Her one room apartment was disgusting, no matter how much she cleaned it, but it was all she could afford. And now she was going to have the added expense of a baby. What the hell was she going to do?

She'd dressed pretty damn sexy prior to her pregnancy because it gave her better tips, but she'd gone back to wearing jeans and tanks. Feeling queasy at all hours of the day made her opt for comfort over looks. She just hadn't felt like squeezing herself into tight shirts and short skirts. Her tips had taken a hit with her wardrobe change, and once she started showing it would be even worse. Her questionable circumstances were about to become dire. Where was her knight in shining armor when she needed him?

A truck pulled up at the curb and a window rolled down.

"Why the hell are you walking?"

She looked over and smiled. "Hey, Griff. You know I walk everywhere."

He grumbled something and then pushed open the passenger door. "Get in before you get robbed, or worse."

She climbed into the truck and closed the door. The werewolf always had good timing. He'd been a friend since high school, one of her only friends for that matter, and he was always bailing her out of trouble. She didn't know what she'd do without him, but even he couldn't help her with her current problem. Last she checked, he couldn't make money grow on trees.

"When are you going to buy a car?" he asked.

"When I can afford one," she retorted. "And trust me, a car isn't at the top of my priority list. If I earned more money, I'd move to a better area before I'd buy a car."

He nodded. "Smart move. You know, the apartment over my garage is still empty."

"We've discussed this before, Griff. I'm not a freeloader."

"So pay rent. I'll take whatever you're paying now."

She snorted. "You know as well as I do that your apartment is worth more than three hundred a month. It might be small, but in that neighborhood you could easily get five hundred for it, or more."

"Look, Sin, I want to help you out. Why won't you let me?"

"I'll think about it."

He nodded. "That's all I can ask."

A few minutes later, they pulled into the parking lot of The Laughing Pig, *the* place to be on a Friday night, other than Luna del Morte. Sin got out and waved to Griff as she entered the bar. They'd only been open a few minutes, but already the regulars were starting to trickle in. She stepped behind the bar to greet Lynox, the bartender and owner, and one of the only were-lions in town.

"Sorry I'm late. I had a rough morning," she apologized.

He grunted. "Still sick?"

She bit her lip. "About that. I'm not really sick."

17

He narrowed his eyes. "Then what are you? You've been puking your guts up every night for a week. If it isn't some kind of stomach flu, what is it?"

"I'm pregnant."

Lynox swore. "Office. Now."

She meekly followed him into the back. When she entered the cluttered office, he closed the door, moved behind the desk and took a seat. She followed suit, easing into the wooden chair across from him. She felt a little like she was being called to the principal's office.

"You know I can't keep you on here if you're pregnant. It's bad for business." He sighed. "You know Alabama is an 'at will' employment state. I could've let you go without even giving you a reason."

She swallowed hard. She hadn't thought of that. "I'm only a month along. Surely I have time before --"

"I'm sorry, Sin. I really am, but I have to let you go." He pulled the checkbook across the desk and opened it. "I'm going to go ahead and give you a full week's pay because I know you need the money."

She nodded, not able to trust her voice just then. What was she going to do? How was she going to pay her rent, her utilities? Her phone bill was due next week and now she wouldn't have money for it. Hell, she wasn't going to have money for food after next week.

"I'll put a word in for you at the Big Bear Diner. I'm sure Mavis can use another waitress, even if it's just part-time. It might not be your dream job, but it will get you by until something better comes along."

"Thanks, Lynox."

"Stop by the diner tomorrow afternoon."

He handed her the check and she accepted it, shoving it into her purse. She rose and went to the door.

"I'm calling Griff to pick you up," he said. "I don't want you walking home, especially not in your condition."

She wanted to argue, but knew it was a battle she'd lose, so she merely nodded and exited before she broke down and cried. She'd worked at The Laughing Pig since she turned twenty-one and had been able to legally serve alcohol. Now, four years later, she was at loose ends.

Once outside, she sank to the ground and rested her forehead on her knees. Nothing in her life ever turned out right. And now she was going to be responsible for someone else. A baby! What the hell was she supposed to do with a baby? She could barely take care of herself.

Griff pulled up in his truck and he got out to help her up. She looked at him with tears in her eyes and he pulled her into his arms.

"Everything will work out, Sin. We'll get you moved into the apartment and --"

"No! I'm not taking advantage of you like that."

He growled. "Damn it, Sin! You have someone other than yourself to think of now. Do you really want to raise a child in that environment?"

"He told you?" she asked softly.

Griff nodded. "And as soon as you tell me who's responsible for this, I'm going to kick his ass."

"Don't. I got myself into this mess and I'll deal with the consequences."

"You didn't get yourself pregnant."

"Maybe not, but I wasn't on birth control so I'm just as much to blame. Okay, so we should've used a condom. It doesn't matter who should've done what. The end result is the same."

Griff shook his head. "Fine. If you want to be a martyr, then we'll lay the blame at your door. For now. But somewhere out there is a guy who's going to be a father, and he has a right to know. Are you honestly going to keep the kid away from his dad?"

She hadn't really thought of it like that. She hadn't really thought about it at all. But something told her Night didn't want to be a dad, especially not if the mother was a one-night stand gone wrong.

"I'll accept your offer of the apartment, but only if I can pay you."

"Fine. But if you're insistent on paying me, I'm going to make sure it's furnished. No way are you bringing any of that crappy secondhand junk to the apartment. That couch of yours had seen better days years before you bought it. And don't even get me started on that lumpy thing you call a bed."

21

Her eyes teared again. She seemed to cry a lot over the past week. It touched her that Griff wanted to take care of her, that he was being so kind and thoughtful. Not that he wasn't always kind and thoughtful, but he didn't have to take care of her. He could leave her to deal with her mess on her own.

When he pulled in to the Silver Moon Storage parking lot, she gave him a curious look.

"We're getting boxes. I'm giving you a day to pack. Day after tomorrow, I'm loading your things in the truck and you're moving into the apartment. No arguments."

"All right."

He looked surprised that she gave in so easily, but smiled.

She waited in the truck while he ran in to get the boxes. She doubted it would take a full day to pack her meager belongings, but it would give her time to say goodbye to the only home she'd known since her parents threw her out after high school. Because of how close she'd been with Griff, they'd assumed something was going on between them, no matter how much Sin assured them that wasn't so.

22

Being snobs, her parents hadn't been able to deal with the thought of their daughter dating a paranormal. If only they could see her now. Knocked up by a werewolf, moving into an apartment owned by another werewolf, and about to go work at a diner owned by a witch and her were-bear husband.

Life was suddenly very complicated.

Chapter Two

Three months later

Oran scanned the crowd at The Laughing Pig. They hadn't been in for months. Shortly after their night with Sin, their alpha had ordered them out of Moonspell to help another pack with a security issue. The issue should have been solved in a week or two, but there had been complications. They'd only arrived back in town last week. They'd come to the bar nearly every night looking for the little waitress, but they had yet to see her. Deciding he'd had enough of looking and wondering, he flagged a waitress in hopes of getting some answers.

"Can I help you?" the little blonde asked with a seductive smile.

"There was a waitress here four months ago. Petite, curvy, short dark hair. She has a tattoo on her back of a cherry blossom tree."

"Oh! You mean Sin. She doesn't work here anymore."

Oran frowned. How in the hell was he supposed to find his mate if she wasn't here? Night wasn't going to be pleased.

"Where did she go?"

The woman shrugged. "All I know is that Lynox fired her about three months ago."

He swore. "Would anyone know where I can find her?"

She nodded toward the bar. "Lynox should know, but I don't know that he'll tell you. He doesn't give out personal information on employees, even when those employees don't work here anymore."

Oran nodded and headed toward the bar, intent on finding the little vixen who had plagued his dreams since their one night together. He'd had several hot little wolves come on to him in Elk Ridge, but none of them had interested him. He wanted Sin and only Sin. And while Night might not admit it, he knew his brother felt the same way. Neither of them had ever been celibate before, not until now. It was the first time either of them had wanted a relationship.

It hadn't gone unnoticed by either of them that they'd been marked during their one night with the hot little waitress, but they'd been too stupid to act on it that night, both caught by surprise. Then, they'd tried to talk to her a few times at the bar and she'd shrugged them off. They'd decided to take a week or two to regroup, and then the call had come from Hayden, telling them they were to leave town for a job. It couldn't have come at a worse time. They'd explained to Hayden about finding their mate, and he'd sympathized but had insisted he needed them to make the trip.

He approached the bar and signaled the bartender.

"What can I get you?" Lynox asked.

"Information. I'm looking for Sin."

He frowned. "She doesn't work here anymore."

"So I heard, but I need to find her. Do you know where she works now?"

Lynox studied him for a minute, his gaze straying to the mark on Oran's arm. "You're one of the guys she went home with about four months ago, aren't you? I'm guessing you got that that night, too."

Oran nodded.

The bartender seemed to come to a decision after a few minutes. "She's working at the Big Bear Diner. I don't know what shift though."

"Thanks. I appreciate it."

Lynox nodded and went back to work.

Oran pulled out his phone and sent a text to Night, letting him know their little sex goddess wasn't at the bar any longer and where they could find her. Taking a chance at finding her this late at night, he decided to make his way over to the diner. If he found her, great. If not, maybe someone could at least tell him when she would be in to work.

* * *

Sin stretched her lower back. It seemed to ache all the time now, along with her feet and swollen ankles. Her belly had gotten big enough that she didn't fit in the standard uniform for waitresses so Mavis let her wear a knit maternity dress. She'd bought two and rotated them so she could wash one each night and have one ready for the next day.

27

The bell jingled over the door and she turned to smile and welcome the new customer, but her smile froze on her face.

Oran looked shocked and then angry. He quickly strode to her side and pulled her out of hearing range of the other customers.

"What the hell? When were you going to say something?" he demanded. "Didn't you think we had a right to know?"

"I figured I wouldn't see you again so it wouldn't be an issue."

He growled. "That's our kid you're carrying. Of course it's an issue. We had a right to know."

"Technically, it's Night's baby. And when you stopped coming to the bar, I figured you weren't interested anymore."

"We both fucked you that night. You belong to both of us, and so does the baby. As for our absence, we had a job to do out of town. We just got back last week and we've been looking for you ever since."

"I don't belong to anyone but myself," she hissed. "If you wanted more than a one-night stand

28

with me, you had several opportunities to say something *before* you left town."

"All right, you have a point. We should've said something and I'm sorry we didn't. I guess we figured we had time. I was content just being near you and I'm sure Night felt the same way."

She didn't say anything. What could she say? This conversation wasn't going the way she'd thought it would. Of course, she hadn't planned on ever seeing them again so she'd hoped to avoid the issue altogether. She fidgeted while she gathered her thoughts. Now that Oran knew, he was sure to tell Night. The question was how would Night react? Would he even care? As much as she'd convinced herself it didn't bother her if the brothers showed an interest in her and the baby or not, she knew she'd been lying to herself.

"I can't talk about this right now. I'm working."

"What time do you get off work?" he asked.

"In about four hours."

He nodded toward a booth in her section in the corner. "Then I'll wait."

She frowned. "You're going to sit there for four hours? Doing what?"

"Watching over you. I don't trust you not to bolt."

She was a little insulted that he thought so little of her. Besides, even if she wanted to run off, she had no way to go home until Griff arrived. Her friend had insisted on playing chauffeur ever since she'd moved in with him. She knew he had to be tired of it by now, but he never complained.

Sin watched as Oran sat down in the corner booth. She went behind the counter and grabbed a cup and a pot of coffee before walking back over to him. After setting the cup on the table, she filled it to the brim.

"You're going to need this if you're going to sit here that long. Besides, Mavis has a rule. You order something or you're out of here."

"Thanks. I'll order some food in a minute."

She nodded and walked off. Had she been paying attention, she would've noticed that he'd pulled out his phone to send a text. If she had, she might have been concerned, more so than she already was. Sin didn't know what she was going to do with one Blaylock brother, much less two.

Going about her business, she assisted customers, refilling coffee cups, taking orders, delivering food until the ache in her back intensified to the point of bringing her to tears. She rubbed at the ache again, but stopped when she felt a large, warm hand take over the task. She sighed in relief and leaned in to the touch, not even caring that a stranger was being so intimate with her. She'd thought the aches and pains of pregnancy would come later when she was much larger.

"When is your break?"

She gasped and whirled around, coming nose to chest with Night. "I already had one."

"You need another one. You can't stay on your feet like this all night."

"It's my job, Night. I make do."

"We'll discuss it later then."

He moved away to join his brother and she released the breath she hadn't realized she was holding. While Oran had been the laid back, fun loving of the two the night they'd shared together,

Night had been serious and had a more commanding presence. She was reminded of that now, watching him stride across the room as if he owned the place. Looking at the two, it was hard to imagine they were brothers. With Night's dark hair and serious countenance and Oran's blond Adonis good looks they couldn't be more different.

She moved behind the counter, hoping to gain her composure. She needed to put as much space between her and the brothers as possible. Sin jumped when another waitress placed her hand on her shoulder. Glancing at Becca, she nearly groaned aloud. Out of all the people to witness her near breakdown, it had to be the young were-fox.

"Everything okay? I noticed you talking to the golden boy and tall, dark, and gorgeous." She cast a covetous glance their way. "Don't suppose they're single?"

She started to tell Becca she could have them, but something held her back. Startled, she realized that she wanted to keep them for herself. What the hell? Hadn't she just been worried about facing them and having to deal with the issue of her pregnancy?

How could she go from being worried about their reaction to wanting them all to herself? She'd never been the jealous type before, but she wanted to tell Becca to back the hell off.

"No, they aren't single. They are very much taken."

Becca sighed. "That figures. I bet their girlfriends are gorgeous."

She grinned. "They only have one."

The waitress's eyes bugged out. "You mean they share?"

"Oh yeah, they definitely share. They share me."

Now where did that outrageous comment come from? Just because they'd shared her once didn't mean they wanted to do it again. She glanced their way. Oran was smirking at her, a sure sign he'd heard her with that super wolf hearing of his. She felt her face flame and turned away. Too late to take it back now.

She hadn't planned on telling anyone that the Blaylock brothers had fathered her baby, but it seemed the proverbial cat was out of the bag now.

There was no taking back her words, even if she'd wanted to. Her and her big mouth.

Becca's eyes flicked down toward Sin's growing belly, then she looked over at the Blaylock brothers again. Without saying another word, the woman went back to work. Sin had a feeling that things had just changed between her and the other waitress, which was a shame. She had few friends in town. Not that she would call Becca a friend per se, but at least they'd been friendly toward one another. Now the woman saw her as competition. Before she'd just been the safe pregnant woman that no one was interested in. Now she had two very hot men that she'd laid claim to. Granted, wolves seldom mated with humans, but that didn't stop women from throwing themselves at them.

Sin glanced at the brothers once more. Being watched was going to grate on her nerves. She was going to be a wreck by the time her shift ended. If only she'd been able to convince them to leave and come back later, but something told her that wasn't going to happen. Now that they'd found her, it seemed they weren't going to let her out of their sight.

* * *

Four hours later, Sin was exhausted and in so much pain she wanted to cry. She had an appointment to see her doctor in the morning and would definitely bring the issue up with her. Surely this wasn't common or women everywhere would avoid pregnancy like the plague.

The bell jingled over the door and she looked up and smiled. Griff walked over to her and hugged her gently.

"You look worn out. Are you ready to go home?"

She nodded. "But I think I have some unfinished business first."

He frowned and looked around. "What unfinished business?"

"The Blaylock brothers are here."

"What do they have to do with…" He cursed. "They fathered your baby?"

She nodded again.

"I should kick their asses."

"You could try," Oran called out.

35

Night stood and moved toward them. "Or we could kick yours. Step away from Sin."

"I don't think so," Griff growled. "Who do you think has been taking care of her while you two have been off playing somewhere? And don't even try to tell me you haven't been fucking anything in a skirt. I know you too well."

Night narrowed his eyes. "It just so happens we haven't."

"All we've wanted is Sin," Oran said. "If you don't believe us, ask the alpha in Elk Ridge. That's where we've been the last three and a half months. Hayden decided to lend our services to their pack."

Griff's stance relaxed. "You still had a week or two to make your move before you left. Why didn't you? You treated her like a whore, someone good enough for a good time that you were ready to toss aside once you were done, no better than the other women in your lives. You knew she was your mate. You would've known that night, so why didn't you say something to her? Why didn't you stop her from walking out?"

Oran looked chagrined, but Night looked ready for a fight.

"We don't have to justify our actions to you," Night growled. "This is between us and Sin."

"Someone has to look out for her best interest."

Sin placed a hand on Griff's arm. She didn't quite know what the whole mate comment was about, but she knew she needed to calm her friend down before he did something stupid. "It's okay. I need to hear what they have to say. They can follow us home; it will be more private there."

"You mean you're living with him?" Oran looked horrified. "You can't just move in with the first wolf who comes along."

Griff frowned. "She didn't. I've known Sin since she was sixteen, and I wasn't about to let her stay in that god awful place she was living in, especially when I found out she was pregnant. It wasn't safe."

"Safe?" She had Night's undivided attention now, and she wasn't sure she liked it.

"She was living in a one-room apartment over off Dover and Cliffhaven."

Night looked furious, but Oran looked surprised.

"Were you trying to get yourself killed?" Night demanded. "That's the worst neighborhood in Moonspell. If anyone is going to get raped or killed, that's where it's going to happen."

"I've lived there since I was eighteen and nothing bad ever happened to me," she said. "Besides, not all of us can afford to live in one of the neighborhoods off Cherry."

She glared at the Blaylock brothers, daring them to question her further. She'd done the best she could on the little that she made working at The Laughing Pig, and Little's Laundromat before that. Without a college education, she wasn't able to land the better-paid jobs. She'd tried for a secretarial job when she'd gotten out of high school, but they'd told her she didn't have the necessary computer skills. She had a feeling her tattoos were a turn off, too. In addition to the cherry blossom tree on her back, she also had an elaborate bracelet on her right wrist. The tree could be hidden, but the bracelet was too large to be hidden by a cuff.

Taking Griff's arm, she led him out of the diner. He helped her into his truck and she watched as the brothers got into a Dodge Challenger. Blue with a white racing stripe, it was a beautiful car. She wondered which of them it belonged to. She figured it was Night's since he slid behind the wheel.

She knew the brothers thought she was living with Griff and not in the apartment over his garage. It would've been easy to correct them, but after the high-handed way they'd handled the situation she decided to let them suffer a little. She knew werewolves could be territorial and it seemed that Oran and Night felt she was their property. It irked her, but at the same time, she wanted to belong to someone. The question was did they want her or the baby? Of course, Oran had come looking for her before he'd known she was pregnant. That had to mean something, right?

"Do you want me to hang around after we get home?" Griff asked.

"Maybe I should talk to them alone. Unless you think they'd get rough?" They didn't seem like the type to hurt a woman, but she didn't really know them.

Griff glanced at her out of the corner of his eye. "They've never laid a hand on a woman. They've been known to fight every now and then, but you'll be safe with them. Especially since you're carrying their child. I imagine they'll treat you like you're made of spun glass." He huffed out a breath. "Besides, there's something more. They're both marked."

"Marked?"

He shook his head. "I'll let them tell you about it."

She wasn't sure if that was a good thing or not. It was one thing to be treated with respect, but she didn't want to be treated like she was going to break. Yes, she was slightly more fragile than she'd been before she became pregnant, but still… she didn't want to be treated differently.

They pulled into the driveway and the Challenger pulled in behind them. Sin took a deep breath, preparing herself for the upcoming confrontation. She'd seen how furious they both looked when they'd discovered her pregnant state and imagined they had quite a lot they wanted to say to her, things she didn't want to hear.

Before she could get out of the truck, her door was opened and Oran was helping her out of the vehicle. Her feet barely touched the ground before she found herself sandwiched between the two brothers. It was a little overwhelming. Pushing against them, she got them to move back a step and give her a little space. Without looking at either of them, she headed for her apartment, not waiting to see if they followed or not.

When she reached the top of the stairs, she unlocked the door and pushed it open, enjoying the cool blast of air that greeted her. She seemed to be hot all the time and the summer temperature wasn't helping any. Most days she felt like she would melt.

The guys followed her inside and closed the door behind them.

"You don't live in Griff's house?" Night asked.

She shook her head. "I rent this apartment from him. I don't pay him nearly enough, but I give him what I can."

"You shouldn't be going up and down the stairs all the time," Oran said with a frown. "It can't be safe in your condition."

She looked down at her baby bump and back up at him. "Are you calling me fat?"

His eyes widened. "No, not fat. It's just, you're... um... pregnant and you could fall."

"I've been managing quite well, thank you."

Oran took her hand. "Why didn't you tell us, Sin? I know we were out of town, but you could have contacted our alpha. Hayden would've gotten in touch with us and let us know what was going on."

"Night seemed so concerned about birth control that night that I figured you wouldn't be interested. I didn't want you to feel trapped. Besides, it isn't like I'm your mate. We can't have a permanent relationship."

The two wolves shared a look.

"What?" she demanded. "What aren't you telling me?"

42

"Did you notice anything that night? Anything unusual?" Night pulled up the sleeve of his T-shirt. "We were both marked. You're our mate."

She frowned. "But I'm not marked."

"If you were, we'd never know. Your back tattoo would cover it up," Night said. "It's quite possible you do bear the mark."

"What happens if I'm not your mate, if you meet her later? I mean, just because the tattoos showed up on you doesn't mean for sure I'm your mate, right? I could've been a fluke or something. I won't tie the two of you down like that. I don't have a problem with you being part of the baby's life, but I think it should end there. Us getting involved again is a bad idea." No matter how much she wanted exactly that.

Night picked her up and carried her to the couch. She was awed by the fact that he could still lift her and didn't fight him. When he sat and settled her in his lap, she sat stiff and unyielding.

Oran sat beside him and caressed her knee. "Baby, we want what's best for you, and right now that's letting us take care of you. And whether you want to believe it or not, you *are* our mate."

"I'm not giving up my independence just because you've decided you need to 'take care' of me. I'm quite capable of taking care of myself. And what I haven't been able to do alone, Griff has handled for me."

Night growled. "He won't be helping you anymore."

"You can't dictate who will and won't help me. It isn't up to you who I'm friends with. Griff has been there for me far longer than I've known either of you, and he'll still be there for me after the two of you are gone. I'm not going to push him aside just because you're territorial. If you don't like my friends, get the hell out of my life and go harass someone else."

"Baby, he didn't mean it like that," Oran said, trying to placate her. "It's just, we want to be the ones to help you. You shouldn't have to rely on someone else when you have us."

She digested that for a moment. The baby was theirs so she supposed she could understand their feelings on the subject, but it didn't mean she had to like it. She'd fought hard for the life she had, and wasn't about to relinquish her independence now. Regardless of what they had to say, she was keeping her apartment. Despite their marks and their assurances, she wasn't convinced she was their mate and she wasn't going to throw away what she'd achieved in the past few years just because they'd decided to dictate her life.

"How about we compromise?" she offered. "I'll let you help me some of the time, go to the doctor appointments with me if you'd like, but you won't pressure me into leaving my apartment or shoving Griff out of my life."

Night and Oran looked at one another before turning their gazes on her. After a minute or two, she had to fight the urge to squirm. Night's gray eyes seemed to look right through her and Oran's green gaze made her want things she couldn't have. If she thought for a moment they loved her, she'd throw herself into their arms and gladly go with them. She knew it was ridiculous to think they'd love her after just one night. Even she wasn't in love. Definitely in lust though. But that wasn't enough reason to throw her life away and jump in with both feet into the unknown with two guys who were known for going through women. If the rumors were true, at least what she'd been able to pry out of her fellow waitresses at The Laughing Pig, neither had ever had a serious relationship and she wasn't sure they were capable of it. And she hadn't lied to them. Not knowing if she was their mate, she wasn't ready to risk her heart. Just because they said it was so didn't mean anything. They could be wrong, couldn't they?

"Only if you agree that we have the right to change your mind," Night said.

"Change my mind?" she asked weakly, having an idea what he meant.

He smiled. "Yeah. Change your mind."

Before she could process what was happening, he leaned down and kissed her, his lips warm and firm against hers. Her heart fluttered in her chest as she sank her fingers into his hair. The voice of reason told her to push him away, but the little devil on her shoulder said it felt too good to deny herself the pleasure of his lips on hers. When his tongue invaded her mouth, she moaned and pulled him closer. The taste of him drove her crazy, made her want to do something rash, like take off all his clothes and lick him from head to toe, beg him to fuck her until she couldn't stand.

She hadn't been with anyone since her night with the two wolves, hadn't wanted anyone else. They'd ruined her for other men with their intensity and passion. Sin couldn't imagine being with another man. But some day, she'd have to get over that. Just not today.

As Night let her come up for air, she realized she was clinging to him like a vine and eased her grip. The look in his eyes was both hungry and tender as he smiled down at her. It was enough to make her want to burrow into him and never leave his embrace, but she had to be strong and stand her ground. She couldn't be weak now of all times, couldn't be swayed by kisses, even if they did make her melt.

"No way do you get to have all the fun," Oran said, pulling her into his arms.

His lips claimed hers, bending her to his will. Where Night's kiss had been tender and loving,

Oran's was full of fire. He drank from her lips as if he couldn't get enough of her. His tongue thrust into her mouth, stroking hers before retreating only to plunge back in again. She wrapped her arms around him and held on tight, not wanting him to ever let go. She was surprised to see this dominant side of him, and liked it.

He pulled back, but didn't release her. If they kept kissing her like this, she had a feeling she'd give in to them before too long. They were just too irresistible.

Chapter Three

"You're overdoing it, Sin. I'm going to recommend that you slow down," Dr. Benson said. "I know you're living with Griffin Humphreys. Maybe he can help out a bit more."

"I'm already asking too much of him. Besides, I'm not living with him, I'm living in the apartment over his garage. And I still have bills to pay; I can't afford to work less hours."

"If you want to keep this baby and have a healthy pregnancy, you're going to figure it out."

Sin nodded, feeling defeated. She knew what she needed to do, and she didn't like it, not one bit. Oran and Night had offered to help her, wanted to take care of her, and it seemed she would have to let them. But first, she needed to talk to Mavis about working part-time; hopefully she could keep her job.

She thanked the doctor and went to the front desk to pay her bill. It was going to drain her bank account, but it wasn't like she could avoid prenatal care. Maybe she should've asked the guys if they wanted to come with her. Honestly, she'd been a little too overwhelmed to even think about it.

After writing the check, she went outside and called Griff. He'd offered to stay with her at the doctor's office, but she'd insisted that she could manage by herself. Mostly, she hadn't wanted him to hover.

It only took five minutes for him to pull up, making her think he'd been window-shopping nearby. There was no way he'd gotten there that fast from home.

"How did the appointment go?" he asked.

"I have to take it easy."

He nodded as if he'd expected that answer. "So what are you going to do? You know I'm happy to let you live in the apartment rent free if that will help any."

"As much as I hate it, I'll have to call Oran and Night. They wanted to help take care of me, well, here's their chance. You know I like my independence but there's only so much I can do by myself, especially if I have to slow down. I got the feeling she wanted me to put my feet up as much as possible."

"I have room in the house if you wanted to move in. I don't mind helping you."

She gave him a tired smile. "Thanks, Griff, but this isn't your problem. Night and Oran got me into this mess. If anyone is going to be saddled with me, it should be them."

He took her hand. "No one is being 'saddled' with you. Don't you know that you're a blessing? Anyone who has you in their home is lucky. And if those two don't realize that, then it's their loss and you shouldn't stay with them a minute longer. Just remember that you always have a place to go. My home is always open to you."

"You've always been like the older brother I never had."

He smiled. "And you've always been the little sister I always wanted. But let's not tell the guys that. It will do them good to keep them on their toes a little longer. I know you're their mate, and they know it, but as long as you're playing hard to get we might as well let them know you have options in your life."

51

Sin laughed. "I already assured them we're just friends."

"Yes, but friendship can always turn in to something more. Me seeing you as a little sister is never going to change."

"Fair enough. If you think it will make them toe the line, we'll leave things as they are."

They pulled into the driveway at home and Sin was surprised to see Night's car already there. She hadn't expected to see either of the brothers for at least a few days. Neither had mentioned stopping by again so soon and she wondered what was up. Surely they hadn't heard about her doctor's appointment. And even if they had, why would they care? It wasn't like anything spectacular happened. Her ultrasound was scheduled for her next appointment.

When she stepped out of the truck and closed the door, Night got out of his car. She admired his broad shoulders and tapered waist as he walked toward her in a long-legged ground-eating stride. Every time she saw him, she remembered why she'd agreed to go to that motel room with him. He was sexy as hell with just enough bad boy charm to be lethal.

He stopped in front of her and studied her a moment, as if looking for just the right words. It made her wonder what he wanted to discuss, what couldn't wait and had him seeking her out in the middle of the day. Surely he was supposed to be at work right now. She realized that she had no idea what he did for a living, nor Oran. Judging by the amount they spent in The Laughing Pig several times a week they had to make a decent amount of money, or they would've gone broke by now. Not at any point in her discussions with the waitresses had they given her even an inkling as to what her two hunky wolves did to make their money.

"Can we talk?" he asked.

She nodded and motioned for him to follow her up to her apartment. Something told her Night didn't want an audience for this particular discussion, otherwise he would've just come right out and said what he came to say in front of Griff instead of asking to speak with her.

After she'd closed the door behind them, she found herself wrapped in Night's arms. Her first instinct was to pull away, but she found that she liked being there. Feeling the muscles through his shirt made her want to rip it off him so she could see his beautiful body. It seemed a shame to hide perfection.

"What did you want to talk about?" she asked after finding her voice.

"Us."

What could she say to that? There wasn't really an "us," but it didn't stop her from wondering what it would be like to belong to the Blaylock brothers, to be their mate. Knowing she wasn't caused her more pain than she wanted to admit to, and okay, so she didn't "know" exactly, but it was a feeling she couldn't shake. Shouldn't they have come to her the very next day after their one-night stand, or even wanted her more than once that night? She felt their need to claim her now had more to do with the baby than anything else. Tattoos be damned.

"There isn't an 'us,' Night."

He dropped to his knee before her and her breath caught in her throat. Pulling something out of his pocket, he showed her a beautiful emerald and diamond ring. Tears gathered in her eyes at the gesture.

"I want there to be an 'us' more than anything, Sin. Oran feels the same way, but since I'm the oldest it was decided that I would be the one to ask for your hand in marriage. Please, marry us. We want to share our lives with you."

She wanted to believe him, she really did, but she had to wonder if he wasn't asking because of the baby. Would he still want to marry her if she wasn't pregnant? A baby wasn't a good reason to get married. What if they tired of her in a month, a year? For that matter, what if she tired of them? Not that she saw that happening, but it was a possibility. Griff had once told her wolves mated for life, but that didn't hold true for all of them, did it? The Blaylock brothers just didn't seem like the one-woman type.

"I can't marry you." He looked like he wanted to argue so she continued. "But I can let you help me more. The doctor said I have to take it easy, which means I'll be working fewer hours. Griff offered to let me stay here rent free, but I get the feeling it's only a matter of time before the doctor puts me on bed rest, at least, if I don't slow down."

He took her hand. "You could move in with us. We'd take care of you."

Sin nodded. "I want to stay on my own, be independent. I earned that right when my parents tossed me out. But I can't do this alone, not with my hours being cut at work. I think moving in with you would be a good idea."

"And you could quit your job."

"No, I can't," she said, shaking her head. "I still have bills to pay even if I don't have a place of my own."

"Let us take care of you, Sin. We'll help pay your bills until you're back on your feet. It's the least we can do."

"And my doctor's visits? Are those included?"

He cleared his throat. "We were actually going to speak to you about that. Since we're the reason you're pregnant, it makes sense for us to pay for your doctor appointments."

Sin wanted to argue, but what he said made sense, and she truly couldn't afford the visits much longer. She'd been stressed worrying about how she was going to pay for her prenatal care, much less cover the expense of the baby's birth. The ultrasound scheduled for her next appointment was going to cost quite a bit, but she was excited about it. Would Oran and Night share in her excitement?

"I'll help you pack," Night said. "We can have you moved as early as tomorrow."

So soon? "Maybe we should slow down a bit."

He cupped her cheek and kissed her gently, his lips a caress against hers. She moved closer and wrapped her arms around his waist, giving in to him. His tenderness was her undoing. This Night was so very different from the one she'd known previously. He deepened the kiss, his tongue stroking hers in a sensual dance.

His hands gently swept down her back to cup her ass, pulling her tight against his erection. The proof of his arousal made her wet, her body preparing to accept him, and she knew she would accept him if he wanted her. Part of her didn't want to leave out Oran, but something told her he wouldn't mind.

Since she was moving in with them, he would get his chance to be with her.

Night tugged her shirt up and over her head, dropping it on the floor. His hands cupped her breasts. They'd been plentiful before, but now they nearly spilled out of her bra. If Night's groan was any indication, he was more than a little appreciative of them. He knelt before her and unclasped the lacy garment and caressed the large mounds, his thumbs flicking over her nipples. Her body responded immediately to his expert touch and she wanted him even more. He took first one in his mouth and then the other, his tongue laving the sensitive peaks.

His hand reverently touched her rounding belly before he placed a kiss there. He looked up at her with a smile, touching the swollen mound before tugging down her jeans, taking her panties with them. Standing bare before him, she felt self-conscious. The last time she'd been naked with him, she'd been tiny. Now she was more than just a little bit pregnant. Would he still want her?

His hands tenderly touched her thighs, moving to her hips. Standing, he pulled her tight against his body and kissed her once more, his mouth demanding. Whatever doubts she'd had fled. Surely he wouldn't kiss her, touch her the way he was, if he didn't desire her.

"You're beautiful," he said.

"Make love to me, Night. I need you."

He divested himself of his clothes quickly then carried her to the bedroom and laid her down on the unmade bed. His heated gaze made her tremble with need. Her lips parted as his body covered hers. Night pressed his lips against her throat and she knew he could feel her pulse pounding. As he left a trail of kisses between her breasts and across her stomach, her nipples tightened, begging for attention. He shouldered her legs apart and settled between them.

Parting the lips of her pussy, he licked her with long, slow strokes. Every time his tongue flicked her clit, her breath caught in her throat. She lifted her hips, wanting more. His tongue delved inside of her before tormenting her again. He lapped at her, his tongue rasping over her clit over and over until she cried out, flooding him with her cream.

Night kissed the inside of her thigh before rising over her. While she was still relaxed from her orgasm, he sank his cock into her pussy inch by inch, giving her time to adjust to his size. She wanted to urge him on, but she loved that he wanted to love her slowly. If she didn't know better, she'd say the look in his eyes was love, but that was ridiculous. They didn't know each other well enough for that.

He moved slowly, using long, deep strokes, driving her mad with desire. She gripped his biceps, needing to touch him, to hold him in some way. Her legs hooked over his, the crisp hair on his legs tickling hers. She felt so very hot and she wanted him more than she'd ever wanted anyone before, even more than the last time they'd been together. The only thing that would make the moment perfect would be having Oran with them.

He leaned down to take her nipple in his mouth, sucking the hardened tip until she arched against him. She threaded her fingers in his hair, holding him to her. As he licked, sucked, and nipped her, she lifted her hips, meeting each thrust, urging him on, needing him harder and faster.

"More," she begged.

Moving to the other nipple, he teased it until it hardened even more. As he tasted her, he plunged into her, giving her what she wanted, what she needed. Her hips bucked against his as she came apart beneath him, crying out his name. As her pussy fluttered around his cock, she felt him come inside of her.

Kissing her, he pulled her into his arms and cuddled her close. She could feel his heart pounding and wondered if hers was keeping time. Their skin was slick with sweat, but she wasn't in any hurry to move. Having Night's arms around her made her feel like she'd come home.

"It occurs to me that my proposal was a bit lacking," he said after catching his breath. "I just sprung it on you out of the blue with no explanation."

"Night, you don't have to --"

"Hush. Yes, I do. I never told you why I was asking you to marry me. It occurred to me that you might think I was asking because of the baby, and while that's a small part of it, that's not all of it.

"I know we don't know each other well, but I missed you while we were gone. I thought about you every day and wished you were in my arms every night. It may be too soon to say anything, but I care about you, Sin. Oran feels the same way. We both want you to be part of our lives."

"But, what if you find your mate?" she asked.

He smiled. "Honey, I'm certain you *are* our mate. I spoke with Hayden and told him how we felt, about the tattoos and what was going on and he said you were destined to belong to me and Oran. While we can get women pregnant who aren't our mates, it's difficult. The fact that you conceived after one time is another indicator."

She allowed herself to feel hope. "So, you really think I'm your mate?"

"We don't think you're our mate, we know it."

She saw the truth in his eyes and knew what her answer would be, the only one that would make all of them happy. She couldn't torment herself any longer, now knowing without a doubt that she was their mate. It changed everything.

"Then, yes. I'll marry you."

He smiled and kissed her. "I promise you'll never regret it. We can meet with the Justice of the Peace as early as next week."

"Whoa, wait. I didn't agree to that. If we're going to do this, I want to do it right. I want a real wedding, with a dress and flowers and everything. I don't think I'm asking too much by wanting that."

Night caressed her cheek. "No, honey. You're not asking too much. I just want you to be ours as soon as possible. How long do you think it will take you to plan something like that?"

"I don't know. Maybe three weeks?"

He nodded. "I can live with that."

They lay cuddled together for another hour before Night shooed her into the shower and let himself out. She wouldn't have minded showering with him, but then that would have led to other things. Maybe he was just anxious to give Oran their news.

Chapter Four

Sin spent the next two weeks planning the wedding. She was so caught up in the details that she almost missed her doctor's appointment. Since it was going to be her first ultrasound and she figured the guys would want to see the baby, she'd called them. Both had seemed eager to join her and had even offered to pick her up.

When a large black SUV pulled up in the driveway, Sin was a little surprised. She hadn't seen Oran's car before now and hadn't known what to expect. The younger wolf helped her down the stairs and walked her to the large vehicle. After helping her inside, he got in and turned to smile at her.

"Are you ready to see if we're having a boy or a girl?"

"I've been ready. Do you know how hard it is to see baby clothes and have to hold back? I didn't want a bunch of white or yellow things."

He backed out of the driveway and they arrived at the doctor's office twenty minutes later, having caught every light between the house and the office. Night met them at the doctor's office and both men escorted her inside and waited with her, rather impatiently. Both wolves seemed to be rather restless and fidgeted constantly. Sin was thankful when they called her name.

Once she was shown to a room and had changed into a gown, the guys hovered. If she'd known they were going to drive her crazy, she wouldn't have told them about the appointment, she just would've shown them pictures. They were both a little intense.

Dr. Benson stepped into the room and smiled at everyone. "I see you brought some people with you this time, Sincerity."

Both guys looked at her with raised eyebrows and she blushed. Her name hadn't come up before now. She knew she should've told them. They were going to find out at the wedding anyway, but the right time just hadn't popped up yet. Her name had always been an embarrassment to her.

"We're her mates," Oran said, shaking the doctor's hand.

If Dr. Benson was surprised, she didn't show it.

"Well, let's see what we're having, shall we?" she asked with a smile.

Both guys moved to where they could see the monitor while Dr. Benson smeared gel on Sin's stomach. When she began moving the wand around, the occupants of the room were in shock. Instead of seeing one baby on the screen, there were two.

"Well, that explains a lot," Dr. Benson said.

"Two?" Night asked.

"It explains why you're a little bigger than most women who are four months along, as well as the fatigue and swollen ankles. Have you been taking it easy like I suggested?"

Sin nodded. "After the wedding next week I'm moving in with Night and Oran. Until then, Griff has been helping out as much as he can, and I cut my hours at work in half."

"Good." Dr. Benson smiled. "Now let's see if we have two girls or boys."

She moved the wand around until she was able to take a good picture of each baby. Handing a picture to Night and the other to Oran, she began wiping the goo off Sin.

"You're having a boy and a girl. Congratulations!"

Sin was still in shock and wasn't sure what to think. It was a little much to process. The fact the babies were healthy was good, but two? What was she going to do with two babies? She wasn't sure she could take care of one!

After Dr. Benson ducked out, Sin got dressed with the guys' help. She wasn't sure she could've navigated the halls to the front desk without their assistance and she waited patiently while Night paid the bill. She was more than a little stunned by the day's revelation. She pressed a hand to her stomach and sent up a prayer of thanks that her babies were healthy. She might not have been expecting two, but at least there wasn't anything wrong with either of them.

Oran escorted her out to his SUV and made sure she was buckled in before he went around to the driver's side. Once he was settled, he reached for her hand, lifted it to his lips and kissed her fingers. She was touched by the gesture and gave him a smile for his efforts. It amazed her how something so small could make her feel better.

"Everything's going to be fine, Sin. So there are two babies instead of one, it just means we have one more baby to love. Nothing has changed, darlin'. We still want to marry you, will be there for you, and will adore our children, however many of them we may have."

Tears sprang to her eyes. "Take me home, Oran. I need to be held and you can't do that in this car."

He grinned. "I think I can handle that, and I'm sure Night will want to join us."

"I'd like that," she said softly. The thought of being held, of being loved, by her two men was comforting. She probably should have asked the doctor if it was still okay to have sex, but surely Dr. Benson would have said something if she needed to curtail her sex life, not that she'd had one until Oran and Night breezed back into her life.

* * *

They barely cleared the door before Night slammed it shut and pulled her into his arms. Oran pressed against her back, placing his hands on her hips. With their heat surrounding her, she felt her pulse race as she contemplated everything they could, and would, do to her. The thought of their lips, tongues, and hands touching every inch of her body made her nipples pucker and her pussy grow wet.

Oran swept her hair to the side and placed his lips against the pounding pulse in her throat. Slowly, he trailed lingering kisses down her slender neck to her shoulder. His hands caressed her hips and gathered the material of her dress, raising the hem inch by inch. While Oran launched an assault on her senses, Night claimed her mouth in a searing kiss, his lips moving over hers with strength and purpose, drawing her into his sensual dance. His hands cupped her face, his thumbs stroking her delicate cheekbones. When his tongue licked the seam of her lips, she opened, welcoming him in, wanting, needing, to taste him.

Night's tongue stroked hers as Oran's hand dipped between her legs, sliding over the satin of her panties. Just that light touch had her spreading her legs for more. She fisted her hands in Night's shirt, needing to anchor herself for fear of floating away. With every swipe of his hand, Oran made her pussy wetter and wetter, making her soak her panties. She knew he had to feel the proof of her arousal, and knew both wolves had to smell it. The thought that they knew what they did to her, that they turned her on unlike anyone before them, made her want them even more.

Oran slipped his hand inside her panties. He eased two fingers inside of her, drawing a moan from between her lips and an involuntary thrust of her hips. The pad of his thumb pressed against her clit as he withdrew his fingers then slid them back in. She bucked against his hand again, wanting more. He stroked her clit, rubbing it back and forth while his fingers plunged inside of her time and again.

Night released her lips to kneel in front of her. Pulling down the top of her dress, he popped the front fastening on her bra, freeing her breasts.

Latching onto one, he licked, sucked, and softly tugged on her hardened nipple with his teeth. She slid her fingers into his hair to hold him to her as he turned to the other side. Every pull of his lips against her breast sent a bolt of pleasure straight to her pussy. Oran curled his fingers as he pulled them out of her, hitting that secret place inside of her, and she came, calling out their names.

Oran lifted her in his arms and carried her into the bedroom, with Night right on his heels. They gave the full-size bed a worried look. She looked at the smallish bed and at the two giants in her bedroom. The bed was barely big enough for her growing body, much less the three of them. She and Night had fit well enough, but Oran as well?

"I know it's small, but... we can make it work, can't we?" she asked.

Oran kissed her. "We'll make it work."

He set her on her feet and began removing her clothes. When he had her stripped bare, he removed his own clothes and backed her toward the bed. She eyed Night over his shoulder and saw that he was removing his clothing in record time. Looking up at Oran, she wondered what he had in mind. Whatever he wanted, she would give him. Twice now she'd been with Night and Oran had only known the pleasure of her mouth. It didn't seem fair somehow.

His hand tenderly cupped her belly. "Are you sure you're up for this?"

She smiled. "I'm sure. The babies are fine, and so am I. You won't hurt either of us. I'm sure Dr. Benson would have said something if we were supposed to abstain."

Leaning down, he kissed her sweetly, his lips softly caressing hers. When he pulled back, she saw heat blazing in his eyes, a flame that burned for her. Night moved around behind her and pulled her onto the bed, her back pressed against his chest as they reclined against the headboard.

"Let Oran love you, honey," Night said as he nuzzled her neck.

"What about you?" she asked.

He nibbled on her shoulder. "I'm going to be right here."

Oran settled between her legs, his cock brushing against her pussy. Her breath caught in her throat, anticipation making her blood race through her veins. He leaned down to kiss her as he eased inside of her. His tongue plundered her mouth as his cock withdrew then pushed back in, a little faster each time. When he began to thrust in earnest, she felt Night kiss her neck and slide his hands up her ribcage. He cupped her breasts, rolling her hard nipples between his fingers.

The feel of Oran's cock sliding into her made her toes curl. The feel of Night's hands on her breasts made her hands grip the sheets. When Night slid his hand down her body until his questing fingers found her clit, she thought she'd expire from pleasure. He pinched and pulled on one nipple while he stroked her clit as Oran pounded into her over and over. Her body was reaching, grasping. Her breath caught and held, and then she was flying! Stars burst behind her eyelids and every nerve felt electrified. As her body began to come back down, slowly relaxing, she felt Oran enter her one last time, calling out her name as he found his release.

Oran kissed her tenderly. "Stay put. I'll be right back."

She heard water running in the bathroom and a moment later he returned with a warm washcloth. After cleaning her up, he returned the rag to the bathroom. She heard water running again and figured he must be cleaning himself, and then he returned a minute later.

Night nipped her ear. "We'll let you rest a few minutes and then it's my turn."

"I want to please both of you at the same time."

Oran lounged beside her, raised on one arm. "Another time, darlin'. We didn't come prepared for that."

Her brow furrowed. "Prepared?"

"He means we didn't bring any lube with us," Night clarified. "We don't want to hurt you. It's going to be uncomfortable your first time even when we are prepared."

"Oh."

Oran caressed her cheek. "We're going to take care of you. If anything we ever do hurts you, all you have to do is say so and we'll stop."

She nodded. Despite the remark about her first time being uncomfortable, she really was rather intrigued by the idea of loving both of them at the same time. She'd heard stories from women at the bar who'd had threesomes, but she'd never wanted to be part of one before, not until the night she'd walked into that motel room with Night and Oran. But then, Night and Oran were different. They were hers forever.

Oran leaned over and kissed her belly. "Hello, babies."

Sin smiled and ran her fingers through his hair. How could she have ever thought to leave them out of their babies' lives? Out of her life? The past two weeks had shown her how caring and tender they could be. They stole kisses every chance they had, carried anything heavier than an envelope for fear she'd injure herself, stopped by the Big Bear during her shift to keep an eye on her… most would consider it smothering, but she knew it was just their way of showing they cared. No one had mentioned love, but she knew she was falling for them a little more each day.

She closed her eyes, feeling content and safe, cuddled by her men. It wouldn't be long before she would fall asleep in their arms every night, and make love with them every chance she had. No room in the house would be safe. She was looking forward to her new life, a life as Mrs. Night Blaylock. While she might be marrying Night, in her heart she would be married to both of them. To her, they were both her husbands.

Night rubbed her arm in lazy strokes and Oran rested his hand over the babies. Unable to deny her body's desire any longer, she allowed herself to tumble into sleep. Somewhere in her mind, she knew she needed to stay awake for Night, but something told her he wouldn't mind waiting. The two incredible orgasms they'd given her had wiped her out.

Chapter Five

Sin woke the next morning alone. She hadn't really expected them to stay in her tiny bed all night, but it would've been nice to wake up in their arms. Pulling the pillows close, she inhaled their scents and closed her eyes. Pretty soon she'd get to wake up surrounded by them every morning, whether they were physically there or not. She couldn't wait!

A glance at the clock showed that she'd slept far later than usual. She only had two hours before work, which gave her plenty of time to get ready and relax. She could check her email on the laptop the guys had given her the week before, using the wireless Internet Griff had installed for her. All of them were spoiling her, and she was really starting to enjoy it. She'd always been independent, getting things for herself, never relying on anyone. But she'd found that by allowing the guys to help her out the past two weeks, she'd freed herself from a great deal of stress and worry. She had never felt so free in her life!

After enjoying a cup of coffee and a Danish, she took a long, hot shower and got dressed. She dried her hair and put on make-up. When she was finished, she looked at her nails forlornly. There wasn't a drop of polish on them, and hadn't been since her stomach had gotten too big for her to reach her toes. She'd thought of going to a salon, but her doctor had warned her against it, claiming the chemicals they used were bad for her during her pregnancy.

A touch on her waist made her shriek and she whirled to face whoever had reached for her. When she saw it was Oran, she relaxed. She had no idea how he'd gotten in, but she was happy to see him.

"You scared me!"

He kissed her, taking his time. "I didn't mean to."

"How did you get in?"

"Griff gave us a spare key last week, in case of an emergency." He grinned. "I decided seeing my girl was an emergency."

Sin leaned into him and rested her head on his chest. "I'm glad you're here."

"What were you doing when I came in?"

"Lamenting my lack of nail polish."

"Your what?"

She looked up and saw the confused look on his face. "I haven't been able to polish my toes since my stomach got to be this size, and there's no point in my polishing my nails if I can't make my toes match."

"Well, we'll just have to do something about that."

"Oran, I may care for you a great deal, but you're not polishing my toes!" Something told her she'd end up with more polish on her feet than her nails.

He chuckled. "No worries, darlin'. I wasn't thinking of me. Our alpha's mate is pregnant and one of the ladies in the pack helps her with things she can't manage, when Hayden isn't around. Like putting on her shoes, painting her nails, fixing her hair."

"Fixing her hair? Why can't she do that?"

"She's due any day now and says she feels like a beached whale. She doesn't stay on her feet for any length of time these days. I imagine you'll be the same way, especially carrying twins."

Sin glanced at her toes and back at Oran. "You'd really get someone to come and paint my nails for me?"

He smiled and caressed her jaw. "Of course I would, darlin'. You just let me know when you're off work and we'll get it set up."

"I'm off tomorrow."

"Then I'll get her here tomorrow."

Sin threw her arms around Oran. He and Night were always doing things for her, but this was different. This wasn't something she really needed, but something she wanted, and he was going to make sure she got it, just like the laptop. She felt so lucky to have the Blaylock brothers in her life; her heart was full to bursting.

"Are you ready for work?" he asked. "I'm your chauffeur today."

She frowned. "Don't you have to work?"

"Not today."

"I don't even know what you and Night do for a living. There really isn't much that I *do* know about you. It hardly seems fair since my life is an open book."

"We own a security company. We provide both security alarms and personal security, which is why we were sent out of town when the Elk Ridge pack needed help. We're the best at what we do, at least, in this area. We have a few other wolves and some cats who work for us. We just recently expanded the company, right before we met you."

"How much security business could you possibly do in Moonspell? We're just a small town."

"Yes, but we're growing every day. More and more shifters are moving here, along with the nest of vampires at the Grant mansion, especially now that they have a new leader. We wired the mansion, as well as the homes of all of the affluent families in Moonspell. And our business is starting to spread to outlying areas."

She was impressed. Here she was a simple waitress and she was marrying two very successful men, men who had worked hard for what they had and seemed to be humble about their accomplishments. After all, she'd had to drag the information out of Oran. At no time had either brother volunteered the information. If she hadn't asked, she probably would've married them not having a clue what either of them did for a job. She still didn't know much about them, though.

"What about your family?" she asked. "You never mention them."

"Mom and Dad died about six years ago. They'd shifted and were running through the woods, but they'd left Moonspell. A hunter in another town shot them. We have a sister, Nara, but we haven't seen her since the funeral. She went home that afternoon, packed her things and left. Night hears from her every now and then, just letting us know she's alive and well, but we have no clue where she is. We figure she'll come home when she's ready."

Her heart went out to him. So much pain. She reached for him, placing her hand on his arm. Giving it a gentle squeeze, she rose on tiptoe to kiss his cheek.

"I'm sorry for everything you've suffered, Oran. You and Night. I can't imagine the horror of finding out your parents had been killed, and then losing your sister, too."

"The hunter went to jail. Since wolves aren't common in this area, the jury decided he should've known they were werewolves. Even though it isn't common knowledge that werewolves exist throughout most of the US, in our area they *are* fairly common. He'll be away for a long, long time."

"Good. I hope he rots in jail."

"Come on. I didn't tell you all of this to make you sad. I want to see a smile and then I'm taking you to work."

She smiled as he'd asked and kissed him, wrapping her arms around his waist. If only she didn't have to go to work! She'd love nothing more than to drag him off to the bedroom and have her wicked way with him. They'd surrounded her last night, left her weak and confused, completely at their mercy. She hadn't stood a chance of getting her way. What she really wanted was to stake him out in her bed and play, have *him* at her mercy for a change. Maybe one day -- soon.

Slipping her hand in his, she allowed him to lead her out of the apartment. They locked the door behind them and Sin carefully maneuvered the stairs, holding on to both the rail and Oran's arm. These days she wasn't taking any chances with her health and safety, especially now that she knew it wasn't just one baby relying on her but two.

Once they were buckled in Oran's SUV and on their way, Sin's stomach rumbled and she realized she'd skipped breakfast. She'd had coffee and then a glass of juice after that, but she hadn't managed to get anything to eat. She'd meant to, but time had gotten away from her. If the look Oran cast her way was any indication, he'd heard and wasn't pleased.

"You didn't eat?"

"I forgot."

He growled. "You can't afford to *forget* to eat! You're eating for three now. I don't care if you're late starting your shift or not, we're grabbing a booth at the diner and you're going to have something to eat. At least tell me you had breakfast."

"Actually, this was going to be my breakfast. I only woke up two hours ago."

Oran gripped the steering wheel. "I guess that's our fault. We shouldn't have worn you out like that."

"Don't you dare apologize for last night! I plan on having many more nights like it. You can't treat me like a piece of glass, Oran. I won't break. And yes, it was bad that I missed breakfast and forgot about lunch today, but it isn't going to kill me. Like you said, I'll eat something at the diner and I'll be fine."

He sighed. "I'm sorry, Sin. I guess I just want to wrap you in cotton and take care of you. You'll have to forgive me if I'm a little overbearing at times. I imagine Night is going to be even worse."

"He definitely hovers when we're together. I'd hoped it would get better the more time he spent with me."

Oran snorted. "Don't count on it. The further along you get the worse it's going to get. And once the babies get here, he'll hover over them until they're able to take care of themselves. You wouldn't think he'd be like that, but he's very protective, to the extreme sometimes."

85

She laughed. "Actually, I can see Night as the protective type. I just didn't expect him to hover quite so much."

They pulled into a parking space at the diner and Oran walked around to help her step down. With his arm around her waist, he guided her up the curb and through the front door. He nodded at Mavis when they walked in.

"Mavis, she's going to be a little late starting her shift. We're going to grab a table and get some food in her first."

Mavis smiled. "That's fine, Oran. You take good care of our girl."

Oran settled her across from him in the corner booth he'd claimed that first night he'd walked in and found her. Having memorized the menu, Sin didn't have to look at it. She ordered quickly when one of the girls came over to take her order and then she went back to staring at Oran. The sun glinted off his hair, making it shine like gold. His kind green eyes made her feel warm and cared for, two things she hadn't felt in a really long time.

"You don't talk about your family much," he said.

"They kicked me out when I was eighteen. There isn't much to tell."

He frowned. "Why would they do that?"

"They thought there was something going on between me and Griff."

"And there wasn't?"

She smiled. "No. We've been friends since the moment we met, but that's all we've ever had between us. I guess because of all the time we spent together, my family decided we were boyfriend-girlfriend. My parents don't like werewolves, or anyone who isn't human, so they tossed me out. Griff gave me the money for my first month's rent and I got a job at Little's Laundromat to pay the bills, until I was old enough to work at The Laughing Pig. You know the rest."

"That's rather bigoted of them. Any reason why they feel that way?"

"I'm sure there is, but I don't know what it is. They never told me, just said I wasn't allowed to date anyone who wasn't human. They didn't even like the fact that Griff and I were friends. And then later, when they thought something more was going on between me and Griff, well… you know how that turned out."

Their food arrived and Sin dug in.

"Well, you have me and Night as your family now."

"And I'll always have Griff."

Oran grumbled.

"You know, your green eyes might be beautiful, but green really isn't your color."

He frowned. "Are you trying to say I'm jealous?"

"Well, aren't you?"

He took a bite and chewed slowly. "Maybe. You have history with Griff and it's obvious the two of you are really close. I know you're my mate, mine and Night's, and that you aren't going to stray, but I don't like the idea of other wolves being around you."

She laughed. "Isn't that a little unrealistic? I will, after all, be around the pack quite a bit."

"Maybe the feeling will die down after you've been ours for a while. The relationship is still new. Maybe that's it."

She smiled. "Maybe."

She ate the last bite of food on her plate and pushed the dish away. Oran had finished a minute before her and was sipping his second cup of coffee. She knew she needed to start working, but she was having a hard time finding the strength to rise and get to it. What she really wanted to do was spend the day with Oran. They'd offered to take care of her bills and let her stay home, and she was certainly going to need to be home with the babies so she was just prolonging the inevitable, so maybe it was time to turn in her notice.

"You seem deep in thought," Oran said.

"It's just... did you and Night mean it when you said you'd take care of everything, financially, if I wanted to stay home?"

He looked surprised. "Of course we did. Why? Are you thinking about it?"

"Honestly, the only thing I want to do today is spend time with you, and if I didn't have to work, I could do exactly that. Instead, I have to work a four hour shift."

"So, quit."

"I can't just leave her high and dry today. I can give my notice, but I'll still need to work at least another week while she finds a replacement."

Oran nodded. "Fine. Give your notice then. But after that, you're ours."

She smiled. "I like the sound of that."

Oran stood and helped her rise. Leaning down to give her a kiss, he brushed his thumb over her cheekbone. "I'll see you in a little while."

Sin watched him walk out, sighing at the lovely view.

Mavis walked over and snapped her fingers in front of Sin's face.

"Girl, are you going to work sometime today, or are you going to drool over that man of yours?"

Sin laughed. "Can I do both?"

Mavis shook her head. "I have a feeling your mind is going to be anywhere but here today."

"About that... I hate to do this to you, but I think it would be best if I stayed home and concentrated on staying healthy and strong for the babies."

Mavis smiled. "I wondered when you'd get around to it. Once those boys came in sniffing around, I knew it was only a matter of time before you quit. If you can come in tomorrow, I can have someone ready to take your place by the day after. There's a high school girl needing some work, but I need to give her notice and get her set up."

Sin took Mavis's hand. "Thank you for being so understanding."

"Don't you worry about it, honey. You just take care of yourself, those babies, and those two hunks of yours."

Sin smiled. "Consider it done."

Following Mavis into the back, she grabbed a pad and pen and began her shift.

Chapter Six

Later in the day, Oran and Night took Sin back to their place. She'd been there twice before, but she still didn't feel quite comfortable in the large home. Well, it was large to her, anyway. She sat on the sofa, cuddled between her men while they watched a movie. As Night placed a hand on her thigh, curling his fingers between her legs, she felt her temperature rise. The simplest touch and she wanted him. It was the same with Oran. A heated look, a caress, and she was mush in their hands.

His hand slid up, shoving her dress further up her legs. Her heart raced in anticipation. His attention was still on the TV, but she wasn't fooled. He knew exactly what he was doing. Night's fingers stroked the inside of her thigh, sending shivers down her spine. Sin forced herself not to squirm.

Oran's arm was around her shoulders and he began caressing the back of her neck, his fingers gently gliding back and forth over the sensitive skin.

Her nipples puckered against her bra as her men teased her. Oran leaned in close, his breath tickling her ear as he whispered to her.

"Have I told you today how beautiful you are?"

She cut her eyes over to him. "No."

He smiled. "Well, you are. Know what would make you even more beautiful?"

She shook her head.

He traced the curve of her ear with the tip of his nose before whispering, "You. Naked. Moaning in pleasure, laid out in my bed. Legs spread, begging for my cock."

Her heart leaped at his words and her breath caught in her throat. She looked at him and saw the desire burning in his eyes, saw his need, a need that matched her own.

Night's hand inched further up her thigh, his fingers brushing against the satin of her panties. That one brief caress sent shockwaves of pleasure rocketing through her body. She pushed her hips forward, wanting more, needing more. His fingers stroked her again and she knew he could feel how wet her panties were.

Oran nipped her ear and trailed soft kisses down her neck, tracing patterns on her skin with his skillful tongue. She wrapped her hand around the back of his neck, holding him to her. He pulled her top and bra strap aside and his teeth grazed the skin on her shoulder. His hand slipped into her hair, anchoring her as he explored.

Night moved to kneel between her legs and eased her panties down her legs. With the bottom of her dress up around her waist, she was exposed to him, her legs open, giving him the access he seemed to desire. He buried his face between her thighs and inhaled her scent before dragging his tongue up the seam of her pussy lips. She trembled with need and buried her fingers in the silky strands of his dark hair.

Oran grabbed the hem of her dress and quickly pulled it over her head, leaving her in nothing but her bra. With a skilled maneuver, he freed her from the garment. Bending his head, he took her nipple in his mouth, his teeth grazing the tip as he sucked hard. Her body bowed, seeking more.

She felt Night's tongue delve inside her pussy before rasping over her aching clit. She gasped from the pleasure and moaned. He pushed her legs further apart as he licked and sucked on her clit, driving her wild. When he thrust two fingers into her, she came on the spot. He gave no quarter, continuing to fuck her with his fingers and that wicked tongue until she came again.

Oran kissed her hungrily, devouring her mouth as his hands teased her nipples. She felt Night bite the inside of her thigh, and then he was gone. Oran pulled away and she looked up at them in confusion, but her unspoken question was answered soon enough. Night lifted her into his arms and began striding toward the back of the house. Depositing her in the middle of a large bed, both brothers began to strip.

Her gaze traveled from one impressive male to the other, her mouth watering at the sight of those long, hard cocks. Knowing they were ready for her, wanted her and only her, made her even hotter and wetter. She beckoned them closer, crawling on her hands and knees to the edge of the bed. With a sultry look, she grasped Night's cock and licked the pre-cum off the head before sliding her lips around him, taking him into her mouth. He groaned and gently cupped her head, caressing yet not holding. He let her set the pace as she swallowed him again and again, her tongue sliding along the steely length of him.

"Christ, Sin. If you don't stop, I'm going to come, and I'd rather be inside of you."

She released him with a *pop* and grinned up at him before turning her wicked gaze on Oran, who was smiling at her, a look of anticipation in his beautiful green eyes. She crawled over to him and gripped the hard length of him. Her eyes remained trained on his as she leaned forward and licked him from base to tip and back again. He hissed in a breath when she took him in her mouth. He was just as endowed as Night, and tasted just as good. Her tongue swirled over him with every stroke until he was panting for breath.

"Sin, stop!"

She pulled back, satisfied that she'd made him as crazy with desire as she felt. Both men were looking at her as if she were something to eat and they'd been without a meal for a long, long time. Sin knew what she wanted, but she wasn't sure if they would agree. She'd been with them several times now, both separate and together, but something was still missing.

"I want both of you. At the same time," she said.

The brothers exchanged a look.

"Are you saying what I think you are?" Oran asked.

She nodded. "I want to feel both of you inside of me at the same time. I'm ready, I know I am."

Night cradled her growing belly in the palm of his hand. "Maybe it isn't such a great idea, Sin. The babies --"

"Are fine," she finished. "It won't hurt the babies, I promise."

Night looked at Oran and nodded. Sin watched as he retrieved a bottle of lube from the bedside table. Night sprawled in the middle of the bed and caught her around the waist, dragging her over his body. When she straddled him, he kissed her.

"Last chance to back out. Are you sure?" he asked.

She nodded. "I'm sure, Night. I want this."

Night lifted her and eased her down on his cock until he was buried inside of her. She shifted her hips, loving the feel of him. No matter how many times they were together, she'd never tire of either man. They were hers, just as she was theirs.

"Lean forward, baby," Night said, tugging her down to his chest.

She lay against him willingly as Oran moved in behind her. She felt the cool lube drip between the cheeks of her ass and then Oran's fingers massaging it into her rosette. Slowly, he eased one finger inside of her, then another. With easy strokes, he thrust in and out of her, and she knew he was taking his time so he wouldn't hurt her.

"More," she said. "I want more, Oran. I want *you*."

She heard him squeeze out more lube and figured he was putting it on his cock, to ease his way inside of her, and then he was there, pressing inside of her, oh so gently. It burned and hurt a little, but she wanted it more than anything, wanted *them*. The head of his cock popped through the tight ring of muscle and then he slid in, not stopping until he was balls deep inside of her.

Sin felt so full, fuller than she ever had before! She wanted to move, to do something, but she didn't know what. Pushing back against Oran, she dug her nails into Night's chest.

"Do something," she commanded.

Night helped her sit up, then placed his hands on her thighs, caressing her. Oran's hands were on her hips as he held her steady. She felt Oran withdraw until just the head of his cock was inside of her snug passage, and as he thrust back in, Night pulled out. In and out, again and again they pushed and pulled, edging her closer and closer to her climax. Oran's grip on her waist tightened as he began thrusting faster and harder, his brother matching him. When she thought she couldn't take it another moment, she screamed her release, coming harder than ever before. She felt both of her lovers come inside of her, felt them panting for breath, and then Oran was withdrawing from her.

He kissed her shoulder as he moved away. "I'm going to get a rag to clean you up."

Night lifted her from his cock and cuddled her close. She felt safe and cherished. Nothing could've prepared her for the experience she'd just had. It was beyond her wildest dreams, more amazing than she could possibly describe. And she wanted to do it again.

"Are you okay?" Night asked.

"I'm perfect," she said with a smile.

Oran returned and cleaned her before tossing the rag back into the bathroom. Climbing onto the bed, he spooned her from behind, resting his hand over her belly. Kissing her neck and her shoulder, he told her without words that he cared for her.

Closing her eyes, she allowed herself to drift, snug and content between her two wolves, her protectors, her loves.

Chapter Seven

The next day found Sin back at her apartment getting ready for work. She'd argued with the Blaylock brothers when they'd insisted she remain with them, and she'd won, explaining that all of her things were still here. She'd be with them soon enough. Eventually, they'd relented.

Dressed in her standard knit work dress, she slipped on her shoes and headed out the door. She was a little early, but thought she'd pop over to Griff's to wait on him. He was her designated driver for the day since both Oran and Night had to work. Locking the door behind her, she placed her hand on the rail and started down the steps. About three steps down, a wave of dizziness hit her and she faltered, her foot catching the edge of the step and sliding off. Her eyes widened in fear as her body started to tumble. Losing her purchase on the railing, she fell down the remaining dozen or so stairs to the hard pavement below. Her head cracked on the bottom step, and she briefly thought about how upset Night and Oran were going to be, right before she blacked out.

* * *

Night felt his phone vibrate against his hip and checked the screen to see who was calling. When he saw Griff's number, he stopped what he was doing to answer the call.

"Sin get off to work okay, Griff?" he asked.

"That's why I'm calling, Night. She must've gotten ready early or something, I don't know. I left the house to go up and get her and found her at the bottom of the stairs. We're at the hospital now."

Night's hand clenched the phone until his knuckles turned white. "We'll be there in a few minutes."

Disconnecting the call, he went to find Oran. His heart was pounding in his chest. Griff hadn't told him much, but the thought of Sin in the hospital terrified him. Just knowing she'd taken a tumble down those stairs was enough to scare ten years off his life. He'd warned her about those stairs time and again, but she'd never listened. They should've forced her to stay the night, should've made her see reason

102

and kept her with them. If they had, this wouldn't be happening now.

He found his brother on the other side of the house they were wiring. When Oran saw him, he flashed him a smile.

"Checking up to make sure I don't cross any wires?"

Night shook his head. "We need to leave. Now."

The smile faded from Oran's face. "Why? What's wrong?"

"It's Sin. She fell down the stairs."

Oran rose and tossed down the wire cutters he'd been holding. "Then let's go."

Night nodded and they hurried out to Oran's SUV. The doors had barely closed before Oran was pulling out of the driveway and tearing off down the street. Night drummed his fingers on his thigh, wishing Oran would drive faster, but he knew his brother was going as fast as he could. He just wanted to hurry up and get there. Griff had been cryptic on the phone, not saying whether or not Sin was okay, if the babies were okay.

It didn't take long before they were pulling into the hospital parking lot. Oran let Night out at the door and went to find a place to park. Rushing through the doors like a bat out of hell, Night found Griff sitting in one of the ER waiting room chairs. He hastened to his side, needing details and needing them now.

"Griff, what have they said?"

Griff looked up, his eyes red-rimmed as if he'd been crying. "She hasn't woken up yet. The doctor wouldn't tell me much, but they're waiting on a room to become available and then they're going to move her."

Night sensed there was more. "What aren't you telling me?"

"There was so much blood, Night. I didn't know what to do. I called 9-1-1, but it felt like it took them forever to get there."

Blood? Night sank into the chair beside Griff, now fearing for his mate's life even more than before. Why weren't the doctors telling them anything? Why hadn't they found a room for her? What was taking them so long, and where the hell was Oran?

104

His brother chose that moment to appear, looking as harried as Night felt.

"Any news?" Oran asked.

"The doctor hasn't said anything yet," Night told him. "All Griff knows is that she hasn't woken up yet."

Oran sat beside Night. "That can't be good. Can it?"

Night shrugged. In his opinion it was bad, very bad, but he didn't want to worry Oran more than the man already was. They sat back and waited, and waited, and waited. Two hours went by before they heard from anyone again. Then a man in scrubs and a white coat came and found them.

He looked at Griff. "Are you the man who brought in Sincerity Parker?"

Griff nodded and motioned to Night and Oran. "These are her mates."

The doctor addressed all three of them. "Miss Parker's hanging in there, but she still hasn't woken. We've moved her to a private room and you can see her when you're ready." He paused.

"What is it, doc?" Oran asked.

"I don't know how to tell you this, but she lost the babies. We did everything we could, but it was just too late by the time she arrived. I'm sorry."

Night's heart seized, his chest aching from the loss. They hadn't known about the babies for long, but he'd looked forward to getting to hold them, to teach them things. He couldn't imagine life without them now. And poor Sin, what was she going to do when she found out?

"I want to see her," he said softly.

The doctor nodded. "Follow me, please."

He led the trio down several halls and up the elevator to the third floor. When they reached Sin's room, Night was horrorstruck by the pallor of her skin, the tubes running from her to machines that were beeping. They could've lost her. Yes, they'd lost their children, but there could be more children. And if for some reason she couldn't have more, they'd adopt if that's what she wanted to do. All that mattered was that she was okay.

Night went to stand beside her and took her hand in his. "Sin, wake up for me, baby."

She didn't move, didn't flinch, didn't do anything except lie there.

Oran took her other hand. Night shared a look with his brother, and he noticed that Oran looked just as crushed as he felt. His gaze strayed to her now flat stomach and he felt his eyes tear. They'd lost so much, surely fate wouldn't be cruel enough to take Sin from them, too.

"Wake up, darlin'," Oran said softly. "Open those eyes for us."

Still nothing.

A throat cleared behind them and Night turned.

"She may be able to hear you, but she's been unresponsive thus far. Head wounds are tricky. She could wake up today, or it could be a week from now," a nurse said as she came into the room. "I take it you're the fathers of the babies?"

Night nodded.

"I'm sorry for your loss."

"Thank you," he said.

"You think she's going to wake up?" Oran asked. "She isn't going to…"

Night could tell that his brother couldn't even finish the sentence. Hell, Night didn't even want to think about it much less discuss it.

"She'll be fine. We had to stitch up the back of her head, ten stitches. And we had to perform an emergency D&C because of the miscarriage, but I don't see any reason she shouldn't wake up soon. If you'd like, I can have some chairs brought in."

Oran nodded. "That would be nice. We aren't leaving until she wakes up."

The nurse smiled. "I'll be back in a few minutes then."

"Come back to me, Sin. I need you," Night said.

Oran caressed her cheek. "I love you, darlin'. Can you wake up so I can tell you that?"

Night looked at his brother in surprise. He'd already decided that he loved Sin, days ago, but he hadn't known when to tell her. He just hadn't realized that Oran felt the same way. Maybe knowing they both loved her would be enough to pull her back.

"I love you, too, baby."

Night leaned down and kissed her cheek, inhaling her sweet scent. If she didn't wake up soon, he was going to go mad.

"Is this Sincerity Parker's room?" a man asked from the doorway.

Night turned. "Yes. Who are you?"

"Forest Winters." He smiled. "Her brother."

Night looked at Oran and back at Forest. "She doesn't have any siblings. She's an only child."

"I meant I'm her real brother. Sincerity was adopted when she was just days old. The Parkers aren't her real family."

Oran inhaled deeply and growled. "Fairy."

Night looked down at Sin in surprise. "She isn't a fairy, we would've sensed it."

"She had her powers blocked when she was born. My family was being hunted and Mother had the queen spell her so she would pass for human. Sincerity never gained her powers, or her wings. I'm here to right that wrong. Her heritage is the only thing that will save her now."

Oran frowned. "Save her? But the nurse said - _"

"I don't believe the nurse," Forest interrupted. "Without her full powers, her body will begin to shut down at this much trauma."

"Why now?" Night demanded. "Why show yourself now? Where were you when she was living in filth in the slums? Where were you when her parents threw her out? Or when she found out she was pregnant and was too scared to tell us?"

"I didn't know who my parents had left her with. I was already an adult when Sincerity was born and was too busy fighting to pay attention to a baby. I've been searching for Sincerity for a very long time. It was only recently that the queen told me where I could find her, except she wasn't there and I had to search some more."

"What can you do for her?" Oran asked.

Forest smiled. "I can unlock her magick."

Night nodded. "Do it."

"I'll need both of you to step away. And you might want to hide your eyes."

Night and Oran moved away and cast their gazes down to the floor while Forest worked. Night had no clue what the fairy was doing, but he heard him speaking in the fairy language and a bright light nearly blinded him. When he could see again, he looked up and his breath caught. Sin's eyes were blinking open.

He wanted to rush to her side, but Oran held him back. "Best if we let them have a reunion, don't you think?"

Night didn't like it, but he agreed.

* * *

Sin opened her eyes and stared up at the face looking down at her, a face so much like her own. Long white hair framed his face, and silvery eyes stared back at her. She recognized him, and yet she didn't. If she'd ever met him before, she would remember.

"Welcome back, Sincerity," he said with a smile. "How do you feel?"

"Fine." She frowned and looked around. "Where am I?"

"Do you not remember what happened?"

She shook her head and then stopped. She remembered falling. Her hand touched her stomach and tears gathered in her eyes. "My babies."

The man took her hand. "There will be others. Many others."

"Who are you?" she asked softly.

"Don't you know? Look inside yourself."

She reached up and traced his cheekbones and his chin. "We're related, aren't we? And yet, I know all of the Parkers and you don't look anything like them."

"That's because we aren't Parkers. You were adopted."

Adopted? That explained so many things. She touched his long, soft hair, exposing his ears and she gasped. The tips were pointed. If he had pointed ears, then… she touched her own. Where they had once been rounded, they now had fine tips.

"What are you? What am *I*?" she asked.

"Fairy. I had to unlock your magick. Your heritage was hidden when you were born, just as you were. But now that I've found you, you don't have to hide who you truly are. And you don't have to be alone. I'll always be there for you."

A tear trickled down her cheek. "I don't even know your name."

"Forest. Forest Winters." He smiled. "And *you* are Sincerity Winters. I was rather surprised the Parkers kept your name."

"You mean my real mother gave me that name?"

He nodded.

"Where is she? Can I meet her?"

Sadness gathered in his eyes. "I'm all that's left, sweetheart. There was a war between our family and another. Everyone was wiped out except for me."

"But... you don't look that much older than me. How did a little boy survive something like that?"

Forest threw his head back and laughed. "So sweet and innocent. I may not look much older than you, but I'm over a hundred years old, sweet girl. I was the youngest, until you. We had three sisters -- Spring, Summer, and Autumn."

She smiled. "Our mother likes seasons, didn't she?"

"Each name fit the fairy rather well."

"What happens now?"

He caressed her jaw. "That's up to you, sweet girl. I'd like to get to know you. Think you can handle having a big brother butting into your life?"

"I'd like that, very much."

Forest kissed her forehead. "I'll leave you to your mates. I know they're anxious to be with you."

Her gaze sought Night and Oran. They both appeared tightly wound and Sin figured Forest was right in his assessment. She squeezed his hand once more before he moved away.

"I'll come see you soon," he promised.

As her brother walked out, she held her hands out to Night and Oran. Both came to her quickly, one on either side.

"You scared us, baby," Night said as he leaned down to kiss her.

"I'm sorry. If only I'd waited --"

Oran placed a finger over her lips. "It isn't your fault. Don't blame yourself for what happened. It was an accident and nothing more."

She swallowed hard. "Does this change anything between us?"

Night's mouth thinned and his eyes narrowed. "Do you honestly think we wouldn't want you anymore just because you lost the babies?"

"It isn't just that. I'm not who you thought I was. I'm not who *I* thought I was."

Oran rubbed her hand with his thumb as his hand tightened on hers. "Darlin', we don't care if you're human, fairy, shapeshifter… none of it matters to us. You're ours and that's all that matters."

She looked from one to the other. "You really mean that?"

Night nodded. "We really mean that. All that matters to us is you getting well and coming home."

"I think I am well. Forest's magick didn't just bring forth my own magick, but it healed me."

"We're not taking any chances. You're staying for at least one night," Oran said.

"All right. One night," she agreed. "Then we go home."

"Our home," Night growled. "You won't be by yourself any longer. Is that understood?"

She nodded. After all, that's where she really wanted to be anyway, at home with her wolves. She'd loved them before, but now, after their acceptance of her newfound fairy origins and the loss of their children, she loved them even more.

Chapter Eight

Sin pulled a batch of cookies out of the oven as her men moved her belongings into the house. She'd been home from the hospital for three days and had finally sent them to gather the last of her things. It was time. The wedding had been postponed because of everything that had happened, but she didn't need to be married to live with them, to know that she wanted to be a part of their lives, to share in the day to day tasks.

Setting the cookies on the cooling rack, she turned the oven off and went in search of Night and Oran. She found them in the living room, trying to squeeze her meager DVDs onto the shelves with theirs and mixing their CDs together. Walking up behind Oran, she wrapped her arms around his waist.

He placed his hand over hers. "How are you, darlin'?"

"I'm good. Better now that you two are home. I have cookies cooling in the kitchen."

Night turned toward her. "Cookies?"

She grinned. "Peanut butter."

She could practically see him salivating at the thought of his favorite treat. She'd made Oran's favorite dessert for dinner last night, a coconut cream pie, so it was only fair that Night get something he wanted, too. Well, other than her. She knew they wanted her. Even though her fairy magick, and Forest's, had healed her, they still refused to do more than hold her at night. The doctor had said three weeks before they could be intimate again, and both men were holding to that.

"You're going to spoil us," Night told her.

"That's kind of the idea."

"Why don't you pack the cookies in a container? I was thinking we'd stop and get some sandwiches and drinks and take them to the park," Oran suggested.

"I have a better idea. Why don't I order some pizzas, and you two can change into something more... comfortable and we'll picnic in the backyard."

118

Night grinned. "I think she's trying to say she wants us to turn furry."

"You can't tell me you don't want to get out in the sun and run," she said, motioning to the large sunlit backyard.

Both men started removing their clothes before she could utter another word, and a minute later a large black wolf and a solid white one stood before her. She ran her hands through their fur. She'd only seen them in their wolf forms once before, a night she'd stayed over before the miscarriage, and she'd missed them. They followed her through the kitchen and she opened the back door, watching them bound outside.

With a smile, she picked up the phone and ordered their lunch. When she was finished, she joined them in the sunshine, stretching out in one of the lounge chairs on the patio. Oran immediately trotted over and sat beside her, placing his head on her stomach. She scratched behind his ears, watching as his eyes drooped shut in ecstasy. Night ran to her side, sliding to a stop. Sin smiled at him and he licked her cheek.

Before she knew what he was up to, Oran shifted and she found herself running her fingers through his hair. He lifted her hand and kissed her palm.

"You know you can be yourself around us, right, Sin?" he asked.

She knew what they meant. Ever since discovering her fairy lineage, she'd been hesitant to make her wings appear. She'd tried it once or twice, but they felt odd. Sin supposed she'd get used to them eventually. Sitting up, she closed her eyes and concentrated. A tingling in her back told her the magick was working, and a moment later, beautiful gold and purple wings sprouted from her shoulder blades.

Oran reached out and gently caressed one. "So beautiful."

"The two of you are awfully accepting of my ears and wings."

He smiled. "And your magick. It's all part of who you are, and I love who you are, Sin." He sobered. "I love *you*, Sin. Very much."

Her breath caught in her throat. "You do?"

120

He leaned forward and kissed her. "Yes, I do."

Night shifted beside her, transforming back to his human self, and took her other hand. "I love you, too, Sin. More than I can ever say."

Tears gathered in her eyes. "You really love me? Both of you?"

They nodded and smiled at her.

With a sob, she threw her arms around them. "I love you, too. I have for a while now, but I was too scared to tell you."

"Never feel like you have to keep something from us," Oran told her. "You can tell us anything, no matter how big or small it may be. We're always here for you, Sin."

She nodded and kissed them both. "The night you picked me up in The Laughing Pig was the best night of my life. I'm glad I found you."

Night tucked her hair behind her ear. "We're glad we found you, too, sweetheart. Our lives weren't complete until you."

She kissed them again and snuggled between her two wolves. She loved them, so very much, and the knowledge that they loved her too filled her heart with joy. Never again would she be alone, never again would she have to feel afraid, because her mates would always be by her side, protecting her, loving her. What more could she have asked for?

Not ready for Moonspell to be over? The saga continues with *Romance in Moonspell*, a new series coming fall 2013 in e-book and print.

The series begins with A Familiar Sin

Bellamy Crawford might be confined to a wheelchair, but that doesn't mean she's a pushover. Yes, her father may run her life a bit. Okay, a lot, but she's still a strong woman. All she needs is someone to accept her, and her animal, for who she is. And then she meets him – Seaton McCullough – the man destined to be her mate! There's just one small problem, Seaton hates cats. As if that isn't enough, someone intends harm to Bellamy.

Keep reading for a taste…

(excerpt is not from a "final" work and may change by publication date)

Seaton McCullough hunkered down outside the dilapidated cabin in the woods, his gaze focused on the front door even as he listened for his fellow trackers to catch up. They'd tracked their prey across five miles, half of which was in a thickly wooded area on the outskirts of Moonspell. Once they'd picked up the scent, it hadn't taken them long to follow the trail. The idiot hadn't even tried to mask his offensive odor, his cologne thick and cloying, with an underlying scent of stale sweat, fear and desperation. It was the fear that stood out most.

If the man thought he was desperate now, just wait until he had three wolves knocking down his door. He'd made a fatal error when he'd absconded with one of the Crawford girls, daughter of the most respected black wing in town. Not that Seaton had had the opportunity to meet the raven shifter himself.

Seaton's gaze shifted, looking over his shoulder as Xander approached on silent feet, silent to a human anyway. To Seaton, his friend sounded like a herd of buffalo crashing about. If it weren't for Xander's exceptional nose, he never would've made it as a tracker. The man was a hulking giant, making it harder for him to blend in when he wasn't in wolf form, and even then he was huge. And yet, he managed to be one of the best trackers the Moonspell pack had, aside from Seaton and their friend Evan, who was lurking somewhere nearby in wolf form.

"'Bout time you showed up," Seaton said softly. "I was starting to think I'd have to come after the two of you."

A wolf edged between them, giving Seaton an annoyed look.

"Evan, you go around to the back; make sure he can't escape. Xander and I are going to go through the front. One of us will nail the bastard while the other checks on the girl."

"What do you know of Ely Crawford's daughter?" Xander asked.

Seaton shrugged. "Only that she's in trouble. He has a passel of them, all teenagers I believe. I'm honestly not sure which one we're after. All I know is Hayden said jump and I asked how high."

Xander snickered. "I think we pretty much all did. He and Ely go way back."

Seaton sighed. "All right. Let's do this."

Evan moved stealthily forward, creeping around the back of the cabin. As the wolf disappeared around the corner, Seaton and Xander approached the door, both men moving silently. Standing on the porch, they could hear a man inside, ranting, screaming, and the softer dulcet tones of a woman. Perhaps Ely's daughter was no young miss, after all.

Seaton gave Xander a nod and the other man kicked the door in, storming into the cabin. Fast on Xander's heels, he watched as his friend chased after the lunatic who'd thought he could capture a shifter, barreling down the hall after him. Seaton scanned the room, his eyes coming to rest on a young woman tied to a bed, her hands and feet bound. Moving quickly, he released her, rubbing the circulation back into her limbs and helping her sit.

Her hair hung in a long braid over one shoulder, brown wisps had come loose and hung in disarray around her face. Her features were delicate, her nose small and pert, her lips full and sensual. Eyes stared up at him the glittering green of emeralds, eyes that tipped ever so slightly at the corners. Cat's eyes. Even in her rumpled state, she was stunning.

"Are you okay?" he asked.

She nodded. "Who are you?"

He grinned. "My name is Seaton, and I'll be your rescuer today. My partner, Xander, is the one who just ran after your captor, and my other partner is around back making sure he doesn't escape."

"My father sent you, didn't he?" she questioned.

"Actually, my alpha did. I believe your father went to him for help."

Her nose twitched. "Wolf?"

"Yeah. Can you stand? We need to get you out of here."

A smile hovered at the edges of her lips. "If you'll just bring my chair over, I'll be happy to get out of this bed."

His brow furrowed. "Chair?"

She pointed across the room. His gaze followed the direction of her finger and noticed a small wheel chair in the corner of the room. He looked at the black contraption then looked at his petite damsel in distress again. Surely she couldn't mean...

"You can't walk?"

"No. I can stand for brief periods of time, but walking is excruciating so I avoid it as much as possible. Even when I do walk, I can't go very far. Across the room is about it."

Instead of retrieving the chair, he lifted her slight weight into his arms and carried her across the room. Gently setting her in the chair, he watched as she settled herself. It still baffled him that someone who looked so perfect would be confined to that wheeled contraption. And a shifter at that! Of course, as a raven she could always fly and didn't really need to use her legs for much, but still, it was horrible to even think about. What would it be like to be trapped forever, never being able to run with the pack? A shiver raked his spine.

Grasping the handles on the back of the chair, he wheeled her through the front door and onto the porch, where he promptly stopped and surveyed the area. How in the hell had her captor brought her here? The trail they'd followed had been over rough terrain, surely he hadn't pushed her chair through that! Her body would be bruised from the bone-rattling force of some of those dips and large tree roots running across the path. He pulled out his phone and turned it back on. Dialing Hayden, he waited patiently for his alpha to answer.

"Do you have her?" Hayden asked by way of greeting.

"She's safe. But we have a problem. I can't get her out of here, not without a vehicle."

"Tell us where you are and I'll bring her father."

Seaton looked around. "We're in the middle of nowhere. I'll turn on the GPS in my phone. Have one of the tech guys track it."

"Done. Just sit tight and we'll be there soon."

COMING FALL 2013

About the Author

Jessica Coulter Smith has lived in various places around the US, from Georgia to California. She currently resides in Tennessee. An author of adult romance and YA romances (under Jessie Colter), she began her writing career as a poet. Her first poem was published when she was 16, but that was just the start. Many published poems later, along with an Editor's Choice Award for "My World is Tumbling Down", she is quickly making a name for herself as a novelist.

When she isn't writing, Jessica enjoys spending time with her family, reading, or going to the beach. She's especially fond of bookstores and Starbucks! Jessica loves to hear from her fans! You may email her at JessicaCoulterSmith@yahoo.com or visit her at her website: http://www.jessicacoultersmith.com.

Printed in Great Britain
by Amazon.co.uk, Ltd.,
Marston Gate.

4235275R00076